THE RANCHER'S UNEXPECTED GIFT

SNOWBOUND IN SAWYER CREEK

LACY WILLIAMS

CHAPTER 1

Delaney Anderson had never done anything this stupid in her life.

Desperation made people do stupid things.

Delaney prided herself on always making the right choice. The smart choice.

How many times a day did she remind Evan to make right choices? How many times had she told him he'd never regret those choices?

She already regretting coming here tonight.

None of that mattered now. All that mattered was finding her wedding ring.

"Can I take your coat?"

The voice from behind startled her into turning. An attendant in a suit had a warm smile and an outstretched hand.

Delaney took a deep breath. Here went nothing.

She let her arms slip out of the full-length coat. Even inside the expansive foyer, cold air seeped around the massive front door and chilled her bare arms and legs.

She wobbled a little on the black heels that matched her cocktail dress. She'd had to borrow both from her friend Sierra, and neither fit quite right.

The heels were tight enough to pinch her toes —a half size too small. The dress's spaghetti straps made her self-conscious that the whole top might pop off. And the length... She never wore anything this short. The skirt ended well above her knees.

But at least she might blend in to the party guests. The Cattlemen's Association Christmas ball was the premiere event of the season here in Sawyer Creek. The Trudeau family had hosted since forever—even a transplant like her knew that. The massive ranch house on the massive ranch boasted a real-life ballroom. Who built a house with a ballroom? The Trudeaus did.

The annual Christmas shindig drew the Who's Who of land-wealthy ranchers and their families, and a smattering of singles who were well-connected enough to attend.

Yeah, she might blend in for a short period.

As long as she didn't run in to her boss. Ex-boss.

She hesitated on the edge of the ballroom, overwhelmed by the sheer number of people.

The Christmas decorations were beautiful.

And a pain to dust. She'd spent hours in here over the last few days, meticulously clearing the kind of fine dust that seemed to seep through the walls on such a large ranch. Polishing the floor that countless feet were now scuffing. Washing the windows.

After tonight, a new maid would have to do it all over again.

Maybe it was a good thing she didn't work here anymore.

Except thinking about her lost wages made her stomach dip precipitously.

If she thought about that too much, she'd find herself drowning in worry. Mired in a bog that had the power to suck her under.

Find wedding ring.

Avoid Cash Trudeau.

Get out.

As long as she kept to the plan, she'd be fine.

Plans made sense to her. Plans kept her going.

For Evan, she could do this.

She stepped in to the ballroom. No one questioned her right to be here. With her hair swept up in the fancy style and her earrings—cubic zirconium—sparkling in her ears, she might look the part.

But she knew how false appearances could be, didn't she?

She remembered taking off the ring to put on some lotion when her hands had been so dry and cracked that she'd been unable to bear it any longer. The cleaning supplies she used dried out her hands terribly, but she'd worn through her last pair of yellow rubber gloves earlier in the week and wouldn't get paid again until after Christmas.

She thought she'd put the ring in her jeans' pocket with plans to stash it in her purse when she had the chance. But when she'd arrived home after the terrible events of the afternoon, the ring had been neither of those places.

She'd spent a half hour combing through her car, walking along the driveway, and searching the tiny bungalow she shared with her son.

The ring was nowhere.

Which meant it must still be at the Double Cross mansion. The one place she'd promised herself she would never set foot on again.

But the ring meant too much. She had to fetch it.

Even if it meant humiliating herself. Even if it meant getting escorted away by the sheriff.

"Hello, there." A man about her age wearing a tuxedo and bolo tie greeted her with a smile.

The predatory kind. The kind of smile she'd learned meant trouble.

"Excuse me." She tried for a tone between cool and abrupt and attempted to skirt the man.

Except he moved to intercept her. "I don't think I know you. Are you new in town?"

A laugh bubbled up. "No." He didn't know her because he moved in a completely different social circle. She cleaned houses for some of the people in this room. If they saw her, they'd likely ignore her, pretend she wasn't here.

People like Delaney were invisible.

"Excuse me," she said again. "I'm meeting someone."

She tried to edge past him, but he grabbed her wrist. "Don't be in such a rush."

She recoiled from the touch, but his hand encircled her like a manacle. He refused to let go.

"Let go," she said fiercely, though she kept her voice low. The last thing she needed was a scene. There would be no recovering if she lost other housecleaning jobs. She *wanted* to be invisible, at least for tonight.

And then she felt a presence behind her. A warm hand closed around her opposite elbow, and she registered a man close by her side.

"I think you'd better let the lady go."

She froze at the voice.

Her ex-boss. Cash.

Instantly, the handsy guy backed off, releasing his hold on her.

Heart beating frantically, its thudding drowning out the party noise, she turned to face him, the motion knocking his hand away. "Please don't touch me."

He didn't seem perturbed by her reaction at all, only smiled an easy smile. "I was just trying to help."

There was nothing predatory about his smile. His was a smile that said he'd humor her for now, but nothing more. His was a smile that said he was someone used to getting his way.

Which she already knew.

The way his eyes crinkled at the corners made her stomach swoop, and that in turn made her words sharp.

"I don't need your help."

His kind of help had fired her earlier in the day.

Doom settled like a black cloud in her stomach. He had every right to throw her out.

She waited for him to demand she leave.

And waited.

CASH HAD EXPECTED to recognize everyone in the room. He'd grown up in Sawyer Creek. He'd been through 4H with half the folks here. He'd known his generation from school, the older generation from hanging out at their houses after high school football or basketball games. The few he hadn't met when he was a kid he knew now from doing business with them.

But he'd never seen this blonde bombshell before.

Her presence here had to be Mallory's doing somehow. Mallory had taken charge of this year's Christmas ball, including the guest lists.

Because Mom and Dad were gone.

Mallory was taking over the Double Cross.

Cash was going back to his old life in Austin.

Tonight, he wanted to forget all of that.

The mystery woman stared at him, the ramrod-straight set of her spine and the light in her blue eyes seemed to ask *what are you waiting for?*

He'd expected another boring party. Chatting, making nice with people he didn't particularly care to socialize with. But here he was, heart pounding like he was back in seventh grade.

From the first glance he'd had of her crossing the ballroom—just a glimpse of her hair pulled back from her face, the graceful curve of her neck—he'd been ensnared.

He'd had to have a look at her face.

One glimpse of her shocking blue eyes and stunning cheekbones and those lips that seemed to hint at a smile… One glimpse and his thrumming pulse had demanded he meet the beautiful creature.

He didn't believe in love at first sight, but his insides were tied up in knots, and adrenaline was pumping. He hadn't felt this alive since...

Since well before he'd received the news about Mom and Dad's accident. Over a year.

He didn't believe in love at first sight, but he couldn't just let this creature walk away. He didn't know if he'd ever been attracted to someone like this, the powerful magnetism that was drawing him to this woman.

He cleared his throat. "At the risk of sounding as lame as that other guy, I don't know your name either. And I'd like to."

Her expression transformed into disbelief. Maybe even past disbelief to incredulous.

She glanced around self-consciously. He didn't know what she was looking for. The party guests were all caught up in conversation.

"Stop patronizing me," she ground out between gritted teeth.

What?

His expression must've shown his genuine confusion, because her disbelief turned into shock.

"You really don't know who I am?" she asked.

"Am I supposed to?"

He was watching her so closely that he saw the blush bloom not on her cheeks, but across her upper sternum. It spread across the exposed skin there, nearly from shoulder to shoulder. Fascinating.

"No," she said with a false sweetness. He'd heard a saccharine tone like that from his sister before. It usually meant it was time to make tracks. "No, we don't know each other at all."

Her tone and the hard light in her eyes made it clear the words were blatantly false. Why would she lie?

And what had he done to offend her? Was it just that he didn't recognize her? He'd swear he had never seen her before tonight.

"If you'll excuse me," she murmured.

"Wait—"

She froze at his command but didn't turn toward him.

If she knew him at all—and somehow he sensed she did, though his brain strained to find the connection—she had to know he wasn't going to give up so easily.

"Has it been a long time since we've seen each other?" That had to be it. Maybe they'd known each other in high school and he simply didn't recognize her.

She smiled, this time without the saccharine sweetness. "Yes. Ages."

She was still lying. He was sure of it. But why?

He shouldn't be this intrigued. He didn't like being lied to, but something was drawing him to her.

Mallory would say it was Christmas magic, but Cash had stopped believing in magic a long time ago.

Maybe it was this woman. Her own brand of magic, tempting him like he'd never been tempted before.

Whatever it was, he couldn't walk away.

"Please. Tell me your name."

Her eyes tracked up and down his face. Looking for what, he didn't know. She finally seemed satisfied, because she offered one wary word. "Delaney."

Delaney.

It was both unique and unfamiliar.

He didn't know a single Delaney.

But he trusted his gut, and it told him she wasn't lying this time.

Delaney.

"You got a last name to go with that?" he asked.

She gave him a cool stare. "Not one that I'd

care for you to know."

He mimed an arrow heading straight for his heart and exploding there.

She didn't crack a smile. Not even the hint of one. Tough crowd.

But he was flying high because she'd cracked once. He knew her name.

"I'm Cash Trudeau." He extended his hand, aiming for a handshake when he really wanted her close. Tucked into the curve of his arm.

Or closer. In his embrace.

She stared at him, once again wearing an expression that said he was a little cuckoo in the head.

He didn't care.

He left his hand there until she relented with a sigh and put her small hand into his.

The first touch was a shock. Not because of the waves of attraction that sent gooseflesh skittering up his arms and down his spine.

Because of the roughness of her hand. It was a worker's hand. Sandpaper skin he usually felt when shaking a cowboy's hand. Not a woman's. Even Mallory, who was as tomboy as they came, used buckets of lotion to keep her hands soft.

Delaney seemed even more self-conscious as she reclaimed her hand.

She seemed flustered, not looking at him directly anymore.

Which was a plus, as far as he was concerned. She wasn't immune to whatever this crazy thing between them was.

"I have to—I really am looking for someone."

She started to walk away.

Everything about her intrigued him. He wanted to know more.

There was no way he was letting her go that easily.

DELANEY'S PULSE was racing as she walked away from Cash.

He didn't know who she was.

The cad.

The jerk.

Obviously, she'd made less of an impression earlier today than she'd thought.

No. No, he was too high and mighty to notice the hired help, that was his problem.

Even so, it made her feel powerless. Less than.

And she hated the feeling.

It reminded her of everything that was wrong with her life.

It doesn't matter.

Evan mattered. And getting her wedding ring back was the only thing she could do for him right now.

She was brushing past a man in a tuxedo when she felt Cash's presence behind her.

Angry tears burned the back of her nose.

Why couldn't he leave her alone?

She was trying *not* to think about what had happened earlier.

And what it meant for her and Evan.

And that was virtually impossible with the tall, imposing rancher breathing down her neck.

CHAPTER 2

Five hours earlier.

Delaney had to go in there.

But Cash was inside.

She stood outside the ranch's pretentious office with the wide oak desk that she practically had to crawl on top of to dust. A wall of picture frames required extra attention, and the trash can tucked behind the desk was always full, which meant she had to trek it down the hall and outside for disposal.

But none of those annoyances really meant anything.

She didn't mind her job, most of the time. It put food on the table and kept a roof over hers and Evan's heads. Her mom had cleaned houses and the occasional office and taught Delaney that she shouldn't be too proud to clean someone else's toilet.

But when she came face-to-face with someone like Cash Trudeau, she hated her job.

No, that wasn't quite right.

She was ashamed.

Maybe she *was* too proud to clean toilets.

This is ridiculous.

Mallory Trudeau ran most of the ranch operations and had given Delaney a long and specific list of what needed to be cleaned. The office was on the list. Delaney had to go in there.

Even if being around Cash made her goosebumps sit up and take notice.

It wasn't as if he'd ever noticed her before. Mama had taught her well. Be discreet when the client is home. If possible, work around their location in the house. Apologize for being in their way.

Grovel, if needed.

There was no use for it.

Cash had been in the office all day. It was the last room on her list to clean. It was Christmas Eve, and she'd worked through lunch, barely stopping to shove a turkey-and-cheese sandwich in her pie hole. She needed to get home to Evan. She had gifts—too few—to wrap tonight, and she was already taking advantage of Sierra, who'd offered to babysit on her holiday from work.

She fortified herself with a deep breath—

Only to freeze when Cash strode out of the office.

The hall light was off, and even though the hallway was illuminated by natural light from the bank of windows at one end, the man didn't seem to notice her at all. He was moving the opposite direction, so it made sense.

Still. It pinched a little.

But Mama would be proud.

She slipped into the room, set her bucket of cleaning supplies near the door, and propped the vacuum against the wall. If she worked quickly, she could be out of here before Cash came back. If he came back. Maybe he was getting ready for the event tonight. Maybe he was done.

She used a rag to dust the picture frames. She didn't have time to be distracted by a younger Cash and his sister Mallory with their parents. Or to wonder what the plush carpet would feel like beneath her bare toes.

Keep working until the job is done.

She still missed Mama. More during the holiday season. They'd never had much, but Mama had always made Christmas magical.

That was her job now. She'd do better to focus on finishing her job here at the Double Cross and getting home to Evan.

She'd moved to the desk, lifting stacks of file folders to dust beneath, when movement from the doorway startled her.

"Who"—the stack slid from her fingers at the startling sharp voice—"are you?"

She tried to grab for it, but the stack slipped out of her reach. She watched it tumble in slow motion, scattering papers and folders across the floor at her feet.

"I'm so sorry," she stammered.

"What are you doing in here?" Cash demanded, striding into the room.

"Cleaning," she said as she squatted, reaching for the nearest paper. What a disaster. Papers had escaped from their folders, and she had no idea what order they should be returned to.

"Stop," he ordered. "I'll fix it."

He knelt over the pile from the corner of the desk, effectively blocking her in.

"I'm really sorry." She left off trying to pick up the papers when he gave her a scathing glare.

But she had to try to fix this.

He flipped over a sheet of paper, put it on top of the desk.

"If you tell me what you're looking for," she said, "I can help set them out."

His frown only grew deeper. He didn't look up from his sorting. "This is confidential correspondence."

It wasn't like she'd asked to sit here and read it.

She shifted, not knowing whether she should attempt to climb over the desk and finish dusting, or keep trying to help. He didn't seem to want her help.

"I think it'd be best if you left," he said. "Does Mallory know you're in here?"

Mallory had sent her!

Delaney stifled the sharp reply that wanted to escape. *Be discreet. Apologize. Grovel.*

No doubt Mama would be at the groveling stage right now, but dropping the papers had been an accident. Delaney swallowed the defensive words rising in her throat.

"I'm not finished with the room." She made a lame gesture at the overfull trashcan.

He pulled the rest of the pile into his huge hands and stood. "Yes, you are. I've got things to do. And now a mess to clean up."

"So do I," she said under her breath.

His head came up sharply. Uh-oh. Had he heard her?

"I'll be quick," she said. "You won't even notice I'm here." She put the most conciliatory tone possible in her voice. She clasped her hands in front of her to hide their trembling. This was a disaster.

"No."

Her pulse pounded like a drum in her ears at his curt answer.

"Mr. Trudeau—"

"Get out."

He still wasn't even looking at her, and now her temper sparked. "Sir—"

"Get out. Unless you'd like to be let go."

Her temper fired hotter. "It's Christmas Eve. You'd fire me on Christmas Eve over an accident?"

He turned his back to her, bending over the desk as he continued to sort the papers.

Think about Evan.

Furious tears burned behind her nose. Her mind raced frantically. What would Mama do? Mama would've never lost her temper in the first place. Would never be in this position.

Oh, crap. Crap, crap, crapity crap.

"Sir, I really—" *need this job.*

"We're done here," he said, his back still to her. "Don't come back."

JUST THINKING about the humiliating events of the afternoon sparked Delaney's temper anew.

What right did he have to fire her? As far as she was concerned, she'd worked for Mallory.

Plus, she hadn't been doing anything wrong. She'd been following Mallory's orders, for goodness sake!

So what if she'd knocked over a pile of papers. That was fixable. Nothing was *ruined.*

And the fact that he didn't even remember...!

She could practically feel steam rising out of the top of her head. Thinking about Evan, about her careful plan for the evening, didn't help either.

Cash was just behind her. Pulling in closer, if the tingles up her spine were any indication.

"Who're you looking for?" He was close enough that his words brushed her ear with warm breath. He didn't touch her again.

"Your sister."

Why had she blurted that? The second they ran into Mallory, Cash would discover her true identity.

But a glance over her shoulder showed Cash's eyes narrow before his expression cleared. "Not sure you'll find her tonight. She's a woman on a mission."

What did that mean?

"Maybe I can help you."

I don't need your help.

The words were right on the tip of her tongue, but for some reason she didn't reject his offer outright.

He was still looking at her with blatant interest. Nothing predatory like the sleazy guy from earlier. Just open interest.

And the memory of how cruelly he'd treated her earlier was still bouncing around the inside of her head.

Along with an idea.

A really crazy, far-fetched idea.

He'd made her feel so powerless, so small.

What if she could make him feel the same? Get revenge?

It wasn't a charitable thought.

It wasn't something she'd normally ever consider.

But she was worn out. Exhausted. Angry. And it was Christmas Eve.

She wasn't even sure if she could pull it off. She was already shocked that Cash couldn't see through her flimsy disguise—bangs brushed back into her hair, really?—and she'd never purposely tried to make somebody fall for her.

But as she imagined him pulling her in for a goodnight kiss and then rebuffing him, laughing in his face... an evil, Grinch-like laugh bubbled up from somewhere inside her. She barely contained it.

He deserved it after how he'd treated her.

And she deserved the satisfaction, didn't she? For all the times she'd been invisible.

She'd never tried to be coy before. But she tilted her head and let herself gaze at him as if she were just as interested as he was.

She saw the subtle surprise that widened his eyes and then the warmth that sparked there.

"I'll find Mallory later. Are you going to ask me to dance?"

CASH DIDN'T KNOW the reason for Delaney's abrupt about-face, but a moment later she was in his arms on the dance floor, and he didn't care what had changed her mind.

She was curved in all the right places, and he felt on fire where his hand touched her waist. He clasped her other hand, resisting the urge to pull her closer. The musical quartet played a mellow version of Silver Bells. His new favorite song.

"I know you didn't grow up in Sawyer Creek," he said. "Where are you from?"

"I grew up in Galveston."

"A beach babe."

Her nose crinkled adorably. "Not really. My family—we didn't have a lot of time to lounge on the beach."

The song changed to something even slower —a rendition of Silent Night—and he used the opportunity to snug her closer in his arms.

She didn't resist.

Her head tilted to one side as she looked up at him. "What was it like, growing up on the Double Cross?"

He didn't even have to think about it. He'd had a movie-perfect childhood and he knew it. "It was great. I learned to ride when I was three. Do you ride?"

She shook her head.

"What? You live in Sawyer Creek and don't ride?"

"I can ride a bike, a motorcycle, even a unicycle," she said proudly. "But I don't know one end of a horse from the other."

He chuckled. "I'd bet you'd figure it out real quick. We should go sometime. Riding."

She shrugged, her attention caught by something across the room. Her glance slid away, over his shoulder for a moment, which allowed him to gaze at her face. She had one freckle by the corner of her mouth. He had the strongest urge to kiss it.

"My dad took my mom horseback riding for their first date," he said.

Her gaze returned to his, a shadow passing behind her eyes.

His stomach tumbled, and he wondered if

maybe he shouldn't have brought his parents into the conversation. Some people weren't comfortable talking about them.

He was fine, though. He rarely got caught by an unexpected wave of grief anymore.

"We should go riding sometime," he said again.

A tiny line appeared in the middle of her forehead. "I thought you were moving to Austin."

His surprise must've shown on his face. He'd been keeping the move under his hat—or so he'd thought.

"Mallory," he mumbled. His sister had a big mouth.

Delaney flushed, that delicate skin on her collarbone turning pink. "Don't blame her. I... Sometimes I overhear things. I don't gossip," she said quickly.

Her flush spread faster.

She intrigued him.

He wanted—*needed* to see her again.

"My plans in Austin aren't a lock," he said as the music ended. It must be the end of a set, because a new song didn't immediately start up.

Around them, couples separated and clapped for the musicians.

He let her go, his hands experiencing a strange feeling of emptiness, a wrongness that traveled all the way up his arms.

Her eyes skittered away. Was she still looking for Mallory? Whatever she needed, he wanted to help her. Then she would be free to focus on him.

It was purely selfish, but he didn't care.

He felt alive again, because of Delaney.

"Yoo-hoo! Ca-ash."

He felt Delaney pull away at the same time someone called for him. He reached out and snagged her hand before she could disappear into the crowd.

This time, she didn't demand he stop touching her, though he could feel tension radiating through her.

He turned to face Mrs. Jefferson and her husband, an older couple who'd been friends with his parents.

"Hello, dear." Mrs. J bussed both his cheeks with a kiss, her cloying perfume settling over him in a cloud. "The *light dusting* we were supposed to get is turning into a blizzard, so I thought we'd better come say hi and then skedaddle."

The older woman patted his shoulder and moved back so that Mr. J could shake his hand.

He felt Delaney's tension in the clench of her hand. Was the snowstorm worrying her?

He let her go only to shake Jefferson's hand quickly, then reclaimed her hand. Where her fingers had been curled against his before, now her palm was damp and limp.

And he was being rude. He'd get the introductions over and when the couple left, he'd reassure her about the roads. If conditions were bad, she could just stay the night here.

They could talk all night long. Get to know each other. Even take advantage of the mistletoe Mallory had strung strategically throughout the house.

Problem solved.

He felt the corners of his mouth lifting as he inclined his head to her. "Do you guys know Delaney?" He suddenly realized she still hadn't given him her last name. But he also didn't want to make things awkward for her. "Delaney, Mr. and Mrs. Jefferson were friends of my parents."

Mrs. J wore a look of confusion.

"We're acquainted," Delaney said quickly. She tried to tug her hand away, but he didn't let go.

Mrs. J's eagle-eyed gaze honed in on their connected hands. Delaney seemed to shrink under the piercing gaze.

"I didn't realize you were working tonight, dear," Mrs. J said.

"I'm not." Delaney responded tightly. The tension she'd carried when he'd first come upon her in the ballroom returned.

What was going on? Working? Was she a caterer or something?

"I really have to—" Delaney pulled hard enough that it was going to cause a scene if he didn't let her go.

He released her hand.

Felt her slip away even as he stayed rooted in place because of the manners his mama had trained into him.

"Cash, do you know who that is?" Mrs. J asked.

He shrugged. "Some friend of Mallory's."

Mrs. J shook her head slightly. "No, she's—"

"Larry just texted me." Her husband looked up from his cell phone. "Bridge over the Coon Creek is slick as all get out. We gotta get home."

Mrs. J nodded but looked back to Cash, concern written all over her face. "Talk to

Mallory before you dance with that girl again."

What?

He didn't know what was going on, but he didn't let anyone butt into his personal life.

He also wouldn't make a scene. He made himself smile politely, and the couple took their leave.

He spun on his heel, scanning for Delaney.

Who, of course, had disappeared.

CHAPTER 3

DELANEY STOOD IN ONE OF THE SIX GUEST SUITES. She'd left the light out. She hadn't been cleaning in here today, which meant her wedding ring wasn't in here.

She'd just needed a place to hide, and the bedroom had been just down the hall from the party.

What was she doing?

Being an idiot, obviously.

She'd allowed herself to get distracted. By Cash.

What had she been thinking, trying to prove something?

All she'd proved was her own idiocy.

The way he'd held her during those two dances... The way he'd *looked* at her!

It was heady, having that much intensity directed at her.

We should go riding sometime.

Her grand—hasty—plan to humiliate the man had been forgotten because of his smoky gaze. She'd been lapping it up like a thirsty puppy. Flattered by his interest. Considered saying yes to his invitation to go riding.

Until the Jeffersons had approached and reality had crashed around her.

Do you know Delaney?

Why, yes. She cleans our house. Scrubs our toilets and picks up the trash we're too lazy to pick up. Does the jobs no one else wants to do.

She'd run before her little charade was revealed. She'd wanted to humiliate Cash, but the joke was on her. Now he'd know just who he'd been holding in his arms. Who he'd been smiling at as if she were the only person in the world.

And she was the one suffering humiliation. Again.

She shouldn't have let herself get distracted. She'd forgotten the one thing that mattered.

Get the ring.

Get out.

Forget about Cash and the warmth in his eyes

when he'd looked at her.

The bedroom door opened, a rectangle of light spilling on the floor.

For one heart-pounding moment, she had the wild thought that Cash had come to find her. Would he confront her again, kick her out?

But it was a slight woman who slipped into the room, closing the door behind her.

She didn't turn on the lights.

Delaney knew the room's layout and had stationed herself across from the hallway door, nearer the bathroom.

She heard movement, the other woman's dress rustling. Then a small cry.

Whoever it was had knocked into the bed. Delaney knew the sharp metal frame beneath the fluffy coverlet, because she'd banged her knee on it before.

"Ouch. Are you okay?" Delaney asked.

There was a beat of silence.

"Yeah. I'm f-fine." The woman's voice broke.

Delaney felt a stirring of compassion.

She stepped to the attached bathroom and flipped on the light, lighting the room peripherally.

Sometimes the overhead light was too much. Didn't she know it?

The woman sniffed, hiding her face in her hands. Poor soul.

Delaney stepped into the bathroom, Sierra's pinchy heels tapping on the tiled floor. She retrieved some tissues from the box where she'd artfully folded the top tissue two days ago.

When she returned to the bedroom, the woman was still right where she'd been before. The soft light illuminated a stunning red dress and heels.

But the dejected set of the other woman's shoulders told it all.

"Th-thanks," she whispered when Delaney handed her the tissues.

Red Dress sat on the end of the bed, dissolving into tears.

Crud. Had Delaney made things better or worse?

She couldn't just leave. Not when somebody was hurting badly enough to leave in the middle of a party. Not when someone was crying like this.

Because a stranger had once sat next to her when Delaney had had her own meltdown.

She sat on the end of the bed next to Red Dress, who couldn't seem to stop crying.

She waited, like the stranger had over a year ago. Prayed that her presence was a comfort.

When Red Dress's tears slowed, Delaney asked, "Is there anything I can do?"

Red Dress mopped her face with the tissues. "I d-don't think so." She hiccuped.

"Can I call someone for you? Your husband? Or boyfriend? Sister? Mom?"

Red Dress laughed through her tears, the sound slightly hysterical. "None of those."

Delaney didn't say anything as Red Dress took several deep breaths. She'd calmed considerably.

"I'll be all right," Red Dress said.

Delaney got a better look at her blotchy, makeup-smeared face but didn't recognize her.

But she recognized the dejection in her expression. Had seen it in the mirror earlier this afternoon.

"Is it man trouble?" Delaney asked gently.

Red Dress gave another teary laugh. "That obvious?"

Delaney sighed. "Just a feeling. I'm having some of that kind of trouble myself."

Seriously, what had she been thinking trying to get close to Cash? He'd proved earlier in the day that they were too different to get along. He'd never even looked at her when he'd fired her.

He’d looked at her when he'd danced with her tonight, but that had only confused things.

"Why does it have to be so hard?" Delaney thought aloud. "Actually, my situation is kinda my fault."

Red Dress sighed. "The man I've been in love with for months just told me about a friend he wants to set me up with."

"Ouch. That sucks."

But Delaney couldn't help wondering. "Did he name this friend, or was it more like, 'I've got this friend...'" She shifted on the bed. "Just curious."

"The latter." Red Dress wiped beneath her eyes with the tissue.

"I don't know your situation," Delaney said, "but this could be a situation where your guy was talking about himself."

"What?" She couldn't be imagining the note of hope in Red Dress's voice.

"Is there any reason he might not want to come on too strong?"

Red Dress considered. "I nanny for his son."

"Aha." Someone deserved happiness for Christmas. Why not Red Dress? "Maybe he wanted to broach the idea without you knowing it was him, to feel things out. Then if you said no, it wasn't an outright rejection."

"I don't know," Red Dress said slowly. "I mean, he did ask me if I was dating anyone. But then he told me about this friend of his. Who was shy." She paused. "He's a widower," she said softly.

It sounded just like a made-for-TV movie.

"So, there you go," Delaney said. "Maybe he was uncomfortable just coming right out and asking you out. There's only one way to find out. Ask him outright."

She saw the skepticism cross Red Dress's face. "I should go home," she said. "I'm pretty sure my makeup is ruined."

"Oh, I can fix that."

Delaney pulled her reluctant new friend into the bathroom.

She rummaged in her purse. "Here we go." She handed Red Dress a packet of makeup wipes. "Those babies will take anything off."

The other woman hesitated before taking them. "I don't even know your name."

"I'm Delaney." She smiled.

"I'm Amber. Nice to meet you."

Amber leaned over the counter as she used the makeup wipe beneath her eyes. She sighed and began scrubbing at her entire face.

"Our skin tones aren't a match, but I think I can fix your eye makeup," Delaney offered.

"I think I'll just go like this. I've taken up too much of your night. You're missing the party."

Delaney grimaced. "Yeah..." Now it was her turn to sigh. "I'm not exactly on the guest list."

The idiocy of her actions hit her all over again.

She'd never have known what it felt like to be held by Cash if she hadn't shown up tonight.

And wouldn't have known what it felt like to miss it.

"And not being on the guest list is why I'm having man troubles."

Amber shook her head, confusion on her expression.

But Delaney just gave her a gentle push toward the door. "Don't worry about me. You go get your guy." At least someone could have a Christmas romance.

DELANEY ALMOST MADE IT OUT.

She hadn't found her ring. It was past time to give up. She'd phone Mallory after the holiday and ask if she could come back and search the house. Tonight was a loss.

She'd skirted the ballroom without running into Cash and had almost reached the front entrance and the foyer where the coat check had been set up.

And then a hand clamped down on her wrist.

"Wh—"

She barely had a chance to look back before the predatory guy from earlier gave her a none-too-gentle nudge in the back. She stumbled in the heels, but he used the momentum she'd already built up to push her into a shadowed hallway.

"Let go of me," she cried out.

She'd only had a glimpse of the ugly gleam in his eyes, but it was enough. She didn't care if she made a scene.

She didn't want whatever ugly thing he was thinking.

He pushed her against the wall, still holding her wrist and now twisting it painfully. "You thought you'd be rid of me that easily? Maybe no one else recognized you all dolled up like that, but I know exactly who you are. We both know you don't belong here."

The words were spoken too close to her face. His hot breath stunk of alcohol, and she saw the slightly wild look in his eyes. She *did* recognize him. Had seen him once when she'd cleaned for his parents. He'd been scruffy and unshaven and dressed like the loser son he apparently was.

And she knew he never would've dared touch her if she'd been one of the high-society women.

You don't belong here.

"Where's your pretty boy rancher to rescue you now?" he taunted her.

"Help!" she cried out. Surely the coat-check attendant could hear. They weren't that far down the hall.

And then his hot, sweaty hand came up to press over her mouth, his wrist pushing her jaw. With his bigger body pressing her into the wall, there was no space, nowhere to go.

She struggled anyway, fighting against his hold. She screamed with his hand over her lower face until her throat and lungs burned. If she could just get one hand loose—

She couldn't breathe—

And then he was gone. He spun away—no, he'd been thrown off of her.

By Cash, who knocked her attacker against the opposite wall. The man's shoulder and head hit with a satisfying thud.

She gasped in a breath, then another. Her windpipe felt as if it were on fire.

"Andy!" Cash roared over his shoulder, and another cowboy in a suit and dress boots rushed from the party.

Delaney felt raw, laid bare. She turned her back, not wanting to be seen, now that her attacker's hands were off of her. She straightened her dress, thankful that the skinny spaghetti straps had held. Adrenaline rushed through her pounding bloodstream. She had to close her eyes against relieved tears—or maybe they were an after-effect of the fear that had nearly immobilized her.

What if Cash hadn't come?

Over the roaring in her ears she heard him speaking, presumably to his friend Andy. "Get this"—expletive—"out of here. I know you're off duty, but if I have to wait on the sheriff—" His voice got lower or maybe her breaths got louder as she tried to contain the sobs that wanted so badly to escape.

I'm okay. I'm okay.

But she couldn't seem to push away from where she leaned against the wall. It was holding her upright. It was a very polite wall.

"Delaney." He was right there behind her, his voice incredibly soft. "Honey, I'm scared to touch you."

She couldn't catch her breath to tell him to shove off. Or to tell him she was okay.

Her emotions were a rioting mess. She didn't want his touch. Did she?

There was a rustle of clothing behind her, and then, "I'm just going to wrap my jacket around your shoulders. Delaney?"

Somewhere, she found the strength to nod.

Warmth stole through her as his man-sized tuxedo jacket slipped over her shoulders. She didn't feel the press of his hands.

His jacket was warm from his body and smelled like him. And she desperately needed to erase the memory of the hot stink of alcohol, so she breathed in deeply.

Just taking the one breath calmed her. A smidgen, but she'd take it.

So she did it again, burying her nose in his lapel.

"Do you need a doctor?"

She shook her head in reply to his soft question. She didn't want anyone else to see her like this, broken and raw.

"Can you turn around at least, so I can see for myself? Please?"

Earlier, she'd imagined his *please,* imagined him begging for a kiss.

This *please,* delivered in a voice so raw and hurt that it made more tears sting her eyes... this *please,* she couldn't deny.

She turned to face him, lifting her chin. Except, she couldn't contain its wobble.

His eyes... he looked as if he were burning up from the inside out. He scanned her face, down her body. Her wrist ached where the attacker had yanked and wrenched it. But she didn't think she'd have other bruises. Except the one on her soul.

"Do you need a doctor?" he asked again.

"I'm—" *fine.* She couldn't get the word out. Her face crumpled, and to her consternation, *she* reached for *him.*

He pulled her in tight, his ranch-strong arms

coming tightly around her. Hers went around his waist, and she pressed her face to his chest.

Right now, she didn't care if he knew her identity. She just needed to be held.

And hold her he did. She hadn't felt protected, cherished like this since Jonah.

Some of the tension that had faded in Cash's embrace returned. What was she thinking?

She backed away, and he quickly let her go.

Cash didn't think of her the way Jonah had. This afternoon, he'd treated her like pond scum.

Her emotions were all over the place. That was the only explanation for caving in to his embrace.

"I need to go home."

Cash's expression filled with concern. "You should probably sit down for a minute. I think the sheriff's office is going to want to talk to you."

"No. No—I don't want to press charges." Her attacker was well-connected. She wasn't. If word got around, she could lose more jobs. With no income, what would she and Evan do?

Cash's eyes were dark. "If you don't, I will. He came into my house and assaulted one of my guests."

Except she wasn't a guest. Not really.

"I think he'd had too much to drink. That's all." Her eyes skipped over his shoulder as she said the words. Yes, the man had smelled like alcohol, but she'd recognized the predatory look in his eyes the moment she'd run into him in the ballroom.

Cash crossed his arms over his broad chest. Without his jacket on, the white shirt he wore stretched over miles of muscles. "Somebody acts that way in a crowded party, no telling what they'll do in a dark parking lot. He'll face this, whether it's you or me who makes it happen."

And to heck with what you want.

That message came through loud and clear. Cash would get his way, even if he had to bulldoze over her.

But where earlier she might've fired back at him, argued, she was too raw and broken to form a single word.

And his macho-man act was just a reminder of who he really was. And how different they were.

She slipped his jacket off her shoulders, shivering a little at the rush of cooler air against her bare skin.

"Thanks," she whispered.

She skirted around him.

CASH DID his best to curb the caveman roaring inside him. *Mine.*

Some jerk had touched Delaney. Hurt her.

Dude was lucky Cash hadn't bashed his face in.

He'd wanted to.

He hoped Andy had knocked his head on the frame of his squad car.

All the adrenaline rushing through Cash's system wasn't helping him here.

Delaney was walking away, heading for the foyer and the coat check.

He'd said something wrong. Watched as her walls had come up, her lashes had flicked down and hidden her eyes from him.

She didn't want to report an assault like that? A few minutes later and who knew what the jerk would've done to her? Who knew what he might do to the next woman?

And Cash didn't think she was refusing in order to protect the guy.

Somehow, she was trying to protect herself.

"Wait," he said. "Please."

But she barely glanced over her shoulder. Her heels now clicked against the tile in the fancy foyer his great-grandparents had built.

She said something to the coat check guy, handed him a ticket and a folded bill.

He should let her go. She was shaken up, but he didn't see any visible injuries. If she said she was okay, he had to believe her, right?

Everything inside him screamed *don't let her go.*

He'd once asked Dad when he'd known Mama was the one for him. And Dad had smiled this secret smile and said *"you'll know."* Cash had been angry, thought Dad was just putting him off.

But what he was feeling tonight was real. He *just knew.*

That he didn't want Delaney to walk out of here. Not like this.

Maybe not ever.

Coat Check Guy had ducked into the rows of coat racks on their rented stands. This might be Cash's only chance.

"Delaney..."

She looked over her shoulder at him. Her eyes were hooded.

He hated putting himself out there. He never took the risky bet. But he also hated the thought of her walking out. "I think we've got something going here, don't you?"

Those moments when she'd been in his arms for their dance had been incredible. Every second was burned into his brain, a sparkling memory for all time.

But when she'd been in his arms just now... something had happened to him. Connected them.

Disbelief crossed her face. She turned to face him directly.

He experienced a moment of doubt at her expression. No. What was between them was real, even if she couldn't admit it yet.

"I'll drive you home," he blurted. That would give him at least another twenty minutes to press his case. The Double Cross was a good ten minutes out of town. With the snow on the road, he'd have to drive slowly and carefully.

"No."

Her refusal rocked him back. He shook his head, felt muzzy as if he'd been punched.

"C'mon. You can't deny there's something between us."

Her disbelief transformed into something more. She stepped toward him, her eyes now snapping with ice. "You don't even know who I am." She laughed a little, but there was nothing funny about it.

She'd been shocked at him earlier. It was clear she was still mad about it.

"So tell me," he said. Because whatever she had to say, he could fix it, if only he knew. "Who are you?"

"I'm the maid you fired earlier today."

Her words didn't make sense to him. The *maid...?*

And then the ugly truth hit him in the face like a two-by-four.

He scanned her up and down. Gone was the woman in slim jeans and a way-too-baggy polo shirt. Gone was the loose ponytail, gone were the shaggy bangs.

In her place was an elegant woman in a hot dress and heels whose hair was mussed from her ordeal.

How come he hadn't seen it before?

Shame rushed over him. Had he even looked

her in the face earlier? He'd been so caught up in trying to fix the mistake he'd made, he hadn't paid close attention to the woman in his way.

"I didn't fire you," he said. Lame. So sue him, he was still reeling.

Her lips parted in extreme skepticism.

Before he could wrap his brain around what she'd said, Coat Check Dude was there, holding out a worn black peacoat. Perfect timing, Dude.

She slid one arm into the coat, but Cash wasn't done. Not by a long shot.

"So what was tonight, then? Did you come here to humiliate me?"

A shadow of guilt chased across her face, but her lips firmed. She definitely wasn't smiling at him. "I lost my wedding ring today. The Double Cross was the only place I've been, so it has to be somewhere in the rooms I cleaned today."

Wedding ring. The hits just kept coming. She was married?

He couldn't breathe as she went on.

"I thought I could sneak through the party without anyone noticing, find the ring, and go home. Believe me, I didn't want to run into *you*."

The way she said the word left no uncertainty about her feelings toward him.

"Did you find it?" he asked hoarsely.

She tied off her belt, not looking at him. Shook her head.

When she looked up, the ice queen from their first—no, second meeting—was back. "If you or Mallory finds it, I'd appreciate a call. I'll come get it." She gritted her teeth as she admitted, "It's important to me."

Of course it was.

She didn't wait for an answer, just turned and walked out the front door, leaving him with a blast of cold in his face and feeling like a fool.

He was an idiot.

CHAPTER 4

CASH STOOD IN DAD'S OFFICE. EXCEPT IT WASN'T Dad's, not anymore. Now it was just *the office*.

From here, he could see the last of the party guests' taillights tracking down the quarter-mile drive to the state road.

The party had wound down quickly after Delaney's departure. The snowstorm had worsened, and folks had been in a hurry to get home.

Mallory had been nowhere to be found. Neither had his buddy Maverick. Cash wasn't worried. Mallory'd been concerned over a horse earlier in the evening. She'd probably dragged Mav down to the barn—or his best friend had dragged himself. The man had a hero complex where Mallory was concerned.

Cash stared at the small, potted Christmas

tree that Mallory had stuck on the edge of the desk.

I'm the maid you fired.

He couldn't get Delaney out of his head.

He let his eyes roam the room, let himself go back to earlier in his memories.

He hadn't fired her. Not really. He'd told her to get out. That wasn't the same thing.

He'd threatened her, though. Been rude. Annoyed that she'd been in his way when he'd lost ten grand in one of the accounting ledgers. Frustrated at the interruption, then at his papers being spilled across the floor. It would take that much longer to put them back in order.

He'd been a jerk. The only reason he hadn't recognized her tonight was because he hadn't looked her in the face earlier.

He could make all the excuses he wanted: he was busy, she shouldn't have interrupted him... but the reality was there.

He hadn't treated her with basic courtesy.

Mama would've tanned his hide.

Dad would've never been in this position. It didn't matter who they were, school janitor, the lowest paid guy at the sale barn... Dad took the time to really talk to everyone he came in contact with. He knew their name and their life story. Dad wouldn't have lost the ten K, either.

Cash had never been able to live up to his old man's legacy.

And it had never bothered him. Not really.

Until now.

His eyes lingered on the last, most recent picture of his parents before they'd died. Dad and Mom had taken a trip to Cancun together that fall. They posed on the beach, arms around each other.

He'd been invited on the trip but had been deep in a coding project and unable to get away from work. At least that's what he'd told himself. He wished he'd taken the time off, gone on the trip. Why hadn't Mallory gone?

They'd been too wrapped up in their lives, hadn't known just how short time was.

He still regretted it.

Emotion surged, and he turned to the desk, swept the stupid pile of folders and papers off the surface. His action sent the papers flying in an arc, then floating crazily to the floor.

Panting, he stood above the mess. Considered sending the little Christmas tree to follow. Or giving the desk a kick.

But he did neither of those things. Instead, he sank to the floor. Putting his back to the sturdy wooden desk, he hung his head, put his hands over his burning face.

He missed his parents. He *needed* them.

And they were never coming back.

Dad would've told him to get off his butt and make things right with Delaney. No matter how much humble pie he needed to eat. He owed her an apology. Maybe two, if his behavior tonight had made her uncomfortable. In his mind's eye, he could still see her, scared and trembling, after he'd pulled off her attacker. That hadn't been Cash's fault, but he'd made no effort to hide his attraction to her. If he'd made her feel one-one thousandth of the same fear that idiot had, he owed it to her to say he was sorry.

If she was married, he'd made a fool of himself all night.

Was she married? She'd mentioned the wedding ring, but the way she'd looked at him, the way she'd felt in his arms on the dance floor… He'd seen through her denial to the attraction she felt.

Married women could run around. He knew

that. But some sixth sense told him Delaney wasn't like that.

Or maybe that's just what he wanted to believe.

Mallory would know. She might not have an employee file on Delaney, but his sister would've done some kind of interview. She had Dad's knack for finding out all about a person.

But Mallory was nowhere to be found.

Cash sighed and started picking up the folders and papers for the second time. Wondering about Delaney didn't change what he needed to do.

As he cleaned up after himself, he swept his hand across the plush carpet, being sure to cover every inch of the floor, even under the desk.

Make things right. He could almost hear Dad's voice.

Delaney had lost something precious to her somewhere in this room. Or somewhere in the house. And he was determined to find it.

DELANEY STUCK the last piece of tape to the last present and pushed the gift beneath the tree. She sat at the foot of the colorfully-lighted tree. It was so late—or early, rather—that her eyes were crossing with exhaustion.

Sitting beneath the tree that was so much smaller than the one in the Trudeau's ballroom made her feel like it was a Charlie Brown tree.

It wasn't. It was a decently full fir that she'd bought from the stock in the grocery store parking lot. Evan had loved it. They'd spent an entire afternoon stringing lights and decorating it. It smelled just as heavenly as a rich person's tree!

She was just being maudlin. Christmas Eve did that to her. At least, it had done so the last three years. First losing Jonah, then Evan's diagnosis and fight with cancer.

She pushed her hair out of her eyes.

She couldn't stop thinking about Cash. The way he'd looked at her when he'd held her on the dance floor.

And the way the light in his eyes had died in those last few seconds, when she'd told him her identity, why she'd come.

It shouldn't matter.

But somehow, it did.

With a sigh, she stood. Her flannel pajama pants were so worn that the pattern had faded.

But they were comfortable. The sweatshirt she'd thrown over her T-shirt was warm enough. She quickly put away the extra wrapping paper and tape and scissors, then snuck to nine-year-old Evan's doorway to peek inside.

She'd developed the habit when he'd been on his first round of chemo. She'd had an intense, urgent need to check on him before she went to bed. Sometimes her worry would wake her in the middle of the night, and she'd sneak into his room to check his breathing.

He'd thrown off the covers from his top half. His pajama shirt had ridden up to show a slice of concave belly. One arm was thrown above his head on the pillow, his expression peaceful in sleep.

She loved him. And oh, how it hurt to watch him go through the illness and the treatments.

For a few moments tonight, she'd let her worries for her son float away on a cloud of imagination. In Cash's arms, she could've been a rancher's daughter, a princess. Someone whose only worry had been what to wear to the party.

Cash's shoulders were wide enough to bear her worries.

The random thought snuck in, and Delaney blinked at her brain's audacity.

The man might've thought he'd been attracted to her before her big reveal, but not now.

She and Evan were on their own. Besides, she didn't need anyone to lean on. She had a good-as-gold best friend in Sierra. And she had herself.

But oh, for a few minutes, she'd wanted...

Cash.

She blinked away the traitorous thoughts and the hot emotion they brought and tiptoed into Evan's room.

She shouldn't, but she climbed into the narrow twin bed anyway, nudging Evan slightly so she didn't fall off the edge. Her son murmured incoherently and rolled to his side, leaving her room to snuggle.

He was probably too big for this, but her mama's heart had been through so much this year. It couldn't be wrong to hold her son close, not when she'd come so close to losing him.

Exhaustion weighted down her bones, but with thoughts of the rancher running through her brain, it was a long time before she fell asleep.

CHAPTER 5

JUST AFTER DAWN, CASH'S BUTT WAS FROZEN TO the Double Cross's utility vehicle bench seat, but he'd made it. He shut off the ignition, the engine ticking in the snow-covered drive in front of the tiny bungalow on the edge of town. Delaney's place.

Covered in snow, it was impossible to tell the state of her yard. The house could use a new coat of paint—but so could two or three others along this street. In the drive, her little compact car was covered in a blanket of snow.

His face was numb.

Technically, the UTV wasn't street-legal. But after a middle-of-the-night rescue of his sister when the farm truck had spun into the ditch, he'd figured the UTV with its huge all-terrain tires was safer than his two-ton truck. Even if it was freezing in the open-air cab.

The sun had just broken the horizon, and the snow had finally stopped.

After he'd delivered Mallory and Mav to the ranch house, he'd set his friend straight about his feelings for Mallory and then watched from a shadowed hallway as Mav had woken Mallory from beneath the Christmas tree with a kiss. He'd walked away before he could hear any private declarations. Mallory could tell him later.

Seeing Mav find the guts to finally claim happiness was like a kick in the pants.

Make things right.

He would.

And if there were any chance he hadn't killed Delaney's attraction by his callous actions, he was going to find out.

First, he had to unstick his hands from the UTV's steering wheel. He flexed his fingers. Even though he'd worn two layers of gloves, his joints were stiff from the cold.

He got out of the UTV hunched over like an old man. It took an embarrassing amount of time to straighten to his full height. He stomped his feet on the squeaky, packed snow, then made his way toward the two steps and the bungalow's front door.

He caught sight of his reflection in the big, square front window. He looked like a mummy. He wore two woolen hats pulled low, a scarf wound around his head, and the bulky coveralls he'd donned over everything else.

He was hoping for a warm reception, but if things went sour, he hoped Delaney would at least let him warm up for a few minutes before she sent him back into the cold.

Nothing was moving this early on Christmas morning. No movement down the entire street. He was the only person crazy enough to be out.

Maybe crazy in love, if Dad was right.

He stood on the stoop, arm raised to knock.

Was this asking for trouble? He didn't know. But he couldn't stop now.

He tapped on the door.

It took long enough for her to answer that he got even more jittery. He felt as if he'd had two too many cups of coffee.

Then the door cracked open, and Delaney peered out. Her bangs were down in her eyes, her face pink and her hair mussed as if she'd been asleep. She wore a faded sweatshirt over equally faded pajama pants.

"Yes?" she asked cautiously.

"Morning."

Her brows bunched together. "Cash?"

He was so bundled up she couldn't identify him.

He reached up and tugged the scarf down so she could see his nose and mouth. "Merry Christmas."

She still held the door mostly closed and now glanced over her shoulder quickly, then back. Spoke softly. "What are you doing here?"

His heart sank. Clearly, someone was inside. The husband?

He kept his voice low, too. "I won't stay long. Brought you something."

He used one gloved hand to pull the other glove off. His hand was shaking from the cold.

Delaney noticed. She peered over his shoulder. "You drove that thing all the way here?"

"Safer than my truck. Just a little colder."

And his mission was important.

She bit her lip, glanced over her shoulder again, and then motioned him inside.

He stepped far enough in for her to close the

door. He fumbled the zipper at his neck, finally catching hold of it and pulling it down far enough to get his hand into his breast pocket. It took about that long for his eyes to adjust to the interior of her house after being out in the blinding snow.

He came up with the wedding ring. A simple gold band with one square-cut diamond.

"Found this and wanted to get it back to you."

Emotion moved through her eyes. She'd kept distance between them, moving away when he'd come in. Now she reached out and took it. Her fingers held a welcome heat, and he saw her flinch at his cold skin.

That was it. He should turn around and go home.

But his feet seemed rooted to the floor.

She stared at the ring, looked up at him. "You found it?"

"Yeah." Wedged beneath a corner of the desk, where it must've fallen when she'd been trying to pick up his fallen papers. He'd combed the entire office using the flashlight on his phone before he'd caught the glint of light off the band.

She didn't need to know all that.

"Thank you," she whispered. But instead of

putting the ring on her left hand, she put it on her right. Why?

Was it possible she wasn't married? But why would she have the ring?

She avoided his eyes, and he imagined that flush spreading across her collarbone.

"Delaney—"

The words to ask were on the tip of his tongue when movement from across the room interrupted him. He turned toward an archway that must lead to the bedrooms.

"Mom?"

Mom.

A boy of about seven in green-and-red plaid pajamas entered the living room. He beelined toward Delaney.

She had a kid. A son.

Heart pounding, Cash realized he'd interrupted their Christmas morning. The tree was lit, presents still underneath. He should go.

The boy came to Delaney, and she lifted her arm to hug his shoulders, pulling him to her side.

He had bright blue eyes, a match for his mom's. His shoulders seemed small and knobby beneath the pajama shirt.

His hair was cropped close to his head. This

near, Cash could see it wasn't by choice. His hair was patchy in a way he recognized from visiting a buddy who'd fought and lost a battle with leukemia.

Delaney's son had cancer.

DELANEY WATCHED the realization enter Cash's eyes.

Her breath caught in her chest. So many times acquaintances, even kids from church, offered innocent comments that were painful for Evan to hear. *What's wrong with him? Is he going to die? My grandma had cancer and died...*

Would Cash?

She was still reeling from his presence. She should take control of the conversation, ask him to leave, but she felt muddled by the shock of seeing him bundled up, the touch of his icy hand. He'd come all this way in a ranch UTV to deliver her ring.

Her heart was pounding and buzzing, while he seemed totally calm.

"Who's this?" he asked with that easy charm.

She couldn't let her guard down. His next question might be about Evan's health.

"This is my son, Evan."

Evan looked up at the man curiously.

"I'm Cash." He didn't add anything like *I'm a friend of your mom's.*

He'd been quietly serious since she'd opened the door, caution in his eyes.

And something that her heart wanted to believe was hope.

Danger, Will Robinson!

Cash shifted his feet. "I've probably interrupted your Christmas morning for long enough."

"We have Christmas pancakes," Evan blurted.

Where had that come from? Evan didn't usually warm up to strangers. He was shy until he got to know a person.

Evan glanced at her, a question in his eyes.

Sometimes, her son was too perceptive for his own good.

"You should stay and eat. Warm up before you go back outside." She made the offer tentatively. Did she want Cash to stay? She didn't know. But based on the half-second touch she'd shared, he must be freezing through.

Cash cleared his throat. "I don't want to cause any problems." He looked down at his feet—or where his feet would've been out of the massive coveralls. "With your husband."

"My dad died," Evan said.

Heat filled her chest. *Thank you, Evan, for blurting it out like that.*

Cash didn't smile like she might've expected last night. His eyes were shadowed. "I'm sorry." There was a pause, and then Cash said quietly, "My mom and dad died last year."

"That sucks," Evan said with a child's honesty.

"Yeah." Cash blew out a long breath, and she swallowed hard at the vulnerability he was showing.

This wasn't the Cash she'd seen yesterday afternoon. Nor the one last night who'd looked at her with such intensity.

Last night she'd been charmed. But now... she felt weak in the knees.

"Come in," she said softly.

"Let me..." He gestured to his coveralls.

She let go of Evan and turned for the kitchen, leaving Cash to take off his layers.

Evan loitered, not hiding the fact that he was watching.

"You've got a lot of clothes on," she heard her

son say as she crossed to the kitchen and breakfast nook off the living room.

"It's cold outside," Cash said. Her ears hurt from how closely she listened for any sign of impatience. None came. "Your mom gonna let you go out and build a snowman later?"

"A snow fort!"

"I said you could go out for a little while," she called over her shoulder as she pulled a carton of eggs from the fridge. She'd had the pancake batter mixed and ready when Cash had knocked. He was a big man. Pancakes wouldn't be enough.

"Mom, if you help, I know we can make a fort."

Cash followed her son into the kitchen in his sock feet. In his jeans and a flannel shirt, she couldn't help wondering, was this the real Cash? Or was it the tuxedo-clad man from last night?

The man was grinning. "Yeah, Mom. You should definitely help."

She faked a whole-body shiver as she lit two burners on the gas stovetop. "I think I'll watch from in here, where it's warm."

"Aw, Mom," Evan mock grumbled. "What about Timmy, from down the street? He could come help me."

"He had a cold two days ago. I don't think it's a good idea."

She didn't have to look over her shoulder to see the dejected slump of Evan's shoulders.

"Can you set the table, please?" She cracked several eggs into a skillet.

Cash said something in a low voice that she didn't catch.

"I can't be around people who are sick," Evan said in his matter-of-fact way. She heard the rattle of the silverware drawer. "My immune system is compromised because of chemo. Sometimes I can't go to school."

She turned, spatula in hand, ready to protect her son if Cash said one thing out of line.

But the rancher wore an expression of compassion. He held out one hand for the tableware. "That sucks," he said, echoing Evan's earlier words.

"Yeah." Evan went to the kitchen island where she'd set out plates earlier. She grabbed an extra from the upper cabinet and handed it to him.

"I'm rusty, but I used to build top notch forts when I was a kid."

Evan's head came up at Cash's words. "Do you think you could—?"

"Evan," she interrupted.

Both males looked at her, Cash looking slightly chagrined.

"I'm sure Cash has other places to get to today," she said.

Evan's excitement died, and she couldn't quite meet Cash's eyes. "Plus, we still have to open presents."

"Oh, yeah!" Evan bounced on his chair. "How could I forget about presents?"

She felt Cash's stare as she turned to flip the pancakes on the griddle and give the eggs a stir.

She didn't know what she was doing. Cash had her all discombobulated. Surely he was heading home after breakfast, right? He probably had plans with his sister, and they probably had friends or extended family...

She wouldn't count on him sticking around, not after how she'd treated him last night.

"What do you think Santa brought you?" Cash asked.

She heard Evan's scoff. "Santa's not real. I've known for a while."

A backward glance revealed Cash's narrowed eyes. "How old are you?"

"Almost ten. How old are you?"

She caught the quickly-masked expression of surprise before she turned back to breakfast.

"I'm thirty-one," Cash said.

"That's pretty old."

She couldn't stop the twitch of her lips.

"It's not that old," Cash said. Then, "I know you're smiling over there."

Her smile grew wider, but she didn't turn around to let him see.

She plated the last two pancakes and grabbed the bowl of scrambled eggs.

"Mom's twenty-eight," Evan said.

"Hey!" Heat spread across her chest again as she moved to the table. She didn't catch Cash's eye as she put the food on the table.

Evan had slid into the seat behind the table, which left her the outside seat. It would be a tight fit at the nook table.

She hadn't thought this through, because Cash's mere size dwarfed their tiny table. Once she sat, she'd practically be in his lap.

"Coffee," she blurted to cover her sudden panic.

She whirled for the upper cabinets, glad she'd put on a pot when she'd snuck in earlier to make the pancake batter.

"Black's fine," Cash said.

She nodded, kept her eyes on her task.

She was making a fool out of herself. She hadn't had a man in her kitchen since Jonah. And Cash was... very much not Jonah. Where her husband had been laid back, mellow, Cash had only to look at her and she felt intensity radiating off of him. This was a man who made his own rules.

When the two cups were poured, she couldn't delay any longer. She set Cash's mug in front of his plate with shaking fingers.

Hesitated at the edge of her seat, hovering there. Why had she invited him in?

"Mom, sit down," Evan huffed. He was spooning eggs onto his plate, oblivious to the interplay between the adults.

Cash held her gaze. "You'd better sit. You're making me nervous."

She laughed, and even she could hear the edge of hysteria in it. "You don't get nervous." Men like Cash would bluster their way through anything. Wouldn't they?

Cash's sock-clad foot nudged against hers. "Wanna bet?"

The vulnerability and honesty in his eyes made her knees weak.

She parked her butt in the seat before her knees got any wobblier.

Oh, Rudolph. What was she doing?

CASH FELT a minuscule bit of relief when Delaney sat.

He was feeling his way here, each step tentative, as if he were making his way through the white-out blizzard they'd had last night. One wrong move and he'd be in the ditch.

He left his foot where it was, the contact with Delaney both energizing and settling him.

She'd okayed him to stay for breakfast, but she didn't want him to build a snow fort with Evan.

That was okay. He'd follow her cues. And see if he couldn't get her to agree to a date—a real date—before he left today.

He dug into the pancakes—one red, one green, both with chocolate chips—and gave a grunt of satisfaction. "Real good."

Evan grinned, a drip of syrup rolling down

his chin. "Mom makes the best pancakes in the world."

"Tastes like it," he agreed.

He caught the slight wrinkle of Delaney's nose. As if she didn't believe them.

"I don't give false compliments," he said.

This time her stare was downright disbelieving. "What about last night?" she asked.

"I meant everything I said." *Everything*. He wanted to see her again, explore this thing that was between them.

Even with the revelations from this morning, he wanted to get to know her better. More so. She was a single mom with a sick kid, making do. He wanted to know her, inside and out.

"You were at the ball last night?" Evan asked curiously.

"It's more of a party than a ball," he said. "And last night was probably the shortest party in history, with the snowstorm cutting everything short."

"Cash owns the Double Cross," Delaney mumbled. Her shoulders straightened and he sensed that saying the words had her itching to put some distance between them, like she had last night.

"Wow, really?" Evan asked.

He didn't intend to let her. He shifted in his seat, inadvertently-on-purpose pressing his knee against hers.

Her gaze came up to meet his, a sharpness to her eyes.

"So you, like, have horses and everything?" Evan asked.

"A few." He chewed and swallowed a bite of eggs. "Your mom told me she didn't know how to ride. You two should come out, and I'll give you lessons."

His eyes grew wide, his expression filled with joy. "Mom, can we?"

Delaney gave Cash a baleful stare. "We'll have to check with your oncologist. Sometimes animals can have harmful germs," she told the boy. Then, to Cash, "Besides, I thought you were leaving for Austin."

He shrugged. "Plans change."

He'd felt unsettled on the ranch without Mom and Dad there. The decision to go back to his job in Austin hadn't been easy, and it hadn't made him felt any more settled.

Last night, for the first time in a long time,

he'd found true north. And that meant that everything else was flexible.

But Delaney gave him a look that was part disbelieving, part something else he couldn't decipher.

Evan scraped his fork through the syrup on his plate. He raised it to his mouth and licked it.

Cash couldn't help smiling. He'd done the same as a boy.

Evan bounced in his seat. "Can we do presents now? Please?"

Delaney shot Cash an uncertain glance.

"I'll do the dishes and make myself scarce," he offered quietly.

Delaney's eyes went wide.

He couldn't find it in him to be offended. "I *can* do dishes. I've been a bachelor for years."

In Austin, he'd had a two-bedroom apartment, a far cry from the sprawling Double Cross ranch house. Small enough that he cleaned up after himself.

Evan pushed past Delaney, which sent her elbow leaning into Cash's arm. He stretched his arm across the back of her chair, living in the moment.

"Wash your hands," she said absently to the boy.

Evan took off.

Which left them sitting too close.

She grabbed the edge of the table and started to get up, but he clasped his hand over hers.

She squeezed her eyes closed. "What are you doing?" she whispered.

"If you want me to go, just say the words," he said, keeping his voice low. "I'm not here to ruin your Christmas."

Her head ducked. "Why are you here?"

"I didn't like how things ended last night."

Her lashes fluttered, and she tilted her chin up slightly. She peered at him.

Which gave him the courage to go on. "I never should've treated you the way I did yesterday afternoon. I don't have a good excuse for my behavior." He paused, the words sticking in his craw. "I'd make a mistake in the accounting ledgers. Something my dad never would've done. It took me all day to find it, and I was frustrated—but that's no excuse. I shouldn't have taken out my frustration on you. I only hope you can forgive me."

For a moment, he thought she'd reject his apology. Then, she nodded slightly.

"I'd like to stay," he said. "Build a snow fort with Evan. Whatever comes after that. But only if you want me here."

She held his gaze, in her eyes a mix of uncertainty, suspicion, and hope.

He found himself caught there, like she was the tractor beam. He couldn't help leaning toward her—

"Mo-om! C'mon!" Evan's call from the living room broke the moment.

She turned her face way, and for a brief moment her cheek pressed against his shoulder.

"Stay," she whispered.

And then she was up from the chair and out of the kitchen.

Leaving him sitting there with a grin on his face.

He heard her and Evan's murmured voices in the living room. He dawdled, sipping his still-warm coffee, not wanting to intrude on these special moments for them. Maybe next year...

Finally, he rose and gathered the breakfast dishes from the table. A trip to the counter and he was stymied for a moment when there was no dishwasher. From where he stood, he could see Delaney sitting cross-legged on the floor in front of the tree. Evan was out of sight, probably across from her.

She glanced over her shoulder, and he smiled. Yes, he'd do dishes by hand. It couldn't be that hard, right?

Minutes later, he'd soaked the front of his sweater, and his fingers were pruny, but he'd scrubbed their plates and silverware to sparkling. The drying rack was almost full—no room for the coffee mugs. No sweat, he'd dry some things and put them away.

Except there was no towel in sight. He started pulling open drawers. Silverware in the first. Junk drawer—he recognized that one. He found the dish towels next, but when he reached for the top one, paper crinkled. What?

A glance into the living room showed Delaney talking animatedly to Evan. Not paying attention. So, nosy busybody that he was, he shifted aside the few towels in the drawer and found a neat pile of medical bills, most of them stamped "past due."

CHAPTER 6

Of course Delaney was aware of Cash rattling around in the kitchen. She couldn't believe he was doing a menial chore like the dishes.

Or that she'd asked him to stay.

Evan exclaimed as he pulled out the small gifts she'd stuffed in his stocking, giving her moments to ruminate.

What was she doing?

Plans change.

Cash's statement, spoken so easily and matter-of-factly, was a reminder of the stark differences in their circumstances.

She juggled numerous cleaning jobs, worked sixty-plus hours each week to put food on the table, keep a roof over their heads and chip away at Evan's medical bills.

Cash came from a wealthy background. His family had money. Now that his parents were gone...? She didn't know details of his financial situation, but someone who could turn down a job because *plans change* was flying in the stratosphere while she was a peon with her feet practically cemented to the ground.

He was making no effort to hide his interest in her. *Wanna bet?* he'd said when she'd argued that he wasn't nervous. The honest vulnerability of his words had hit her hard.

She made him nervous.

She hadn't been able to quench her attraction to Cash, even when she'd known better than to act on it.

She'd been flustered, flattered when he'd shown up this morning. He'd braved the cold weather. The roads weren't even passable, yet he'd found a way to get to her, to return her ring.

And to apologize. He'd been sincere and serious in his apology. He'd meant it. He'd been vulnerable and brought up his conflicted feelings about his dad.

He'd done everything right, but that didn't mean things could work between them. Attraction was fine, but what about when reality intruded?

She scheduled her jobs around Evan's doctors appointments. When she wasn't toting her son to Austin for treatments or check-ups, she was helping with math homework or trying to catch up on household chores.

Her life wasn't conducive to dating. And when Cash figured that out, he'd lose interest.

And if she let herself fall for him, losing him just might break her.

She didn't know if she had it in her to take that risk.

"Whoohoo!" Evan reached the toe of his stocking and found the pack of Pokémon cards she'd stuffed in the bottom. "Awesome, Mom!"

He ripped into the package, spilling cards across the floor. She laughed a little as Evan scrambled to pick them up, sorting through them quickly.

She swallowed hard. She didn't just have herself to think about. If she allowed Cash into their lives and the relationship didn't make it, Evan could be heartbroken, too.

There were so many things stacked against them.

She sensed Cash's overwhelming presence and glanced up to find him in the kitchen archway, one shoulder against the jamb, his legs crossed at the ankles. He was smiling at Evan's antics, a soft smile that reminded her of Jonah with a pang. A dad's affection.

He was relaxed, very much at home in her tiny house, in her world.

It was she who was overly conscious of the small pile of gifts unwrapped beneath the tree, of her decor that was a decade out of date, and of the paint peeling in the corner of the ceiling.

Cash's Christmases must have been so different from this.

His gaze shifted to hers, and the warmth in his eyes changed, sparked.

Something inside her responded, twisting her stomach into a knot and floating at the same time.

She should tell him to go home.

But she didn't want to.

Evan threw his arms around her, and she tucked her chin into the hug. There'd been a point months ago when she hadn't been sure he'd make it to see this Christmas. She was so very grateful to have him here.

"Mom, can I please go outside now?"

She laughed a soggy laugh as Evan pushed back from the embrace.

"Don't you want to play with your new toys?" she asked.

He eyed the remote-control racetrack in its box. It'd been the only large thing beneath the tree, the costliest gift.

"But the snow's gonna melt. Please?"

She glanced at Cash, who watched with twitching lips. She shrugged. "Not for very long. Bundle up!" she called after him as he dashed toward his bedroom.

She stood, self-conscious that she was still in her PJs. She brushed a hank of hair out of her face.

"Is it dangerous for him to be outside?" Cash asked.

"Like he said, the chemo makes his immune system weak. Most doctors believe cold weather suppresses the immune system, too, but he's on winter break, so he won't be around other kids and germs, and I don't think being outside for a half hour will hurt him."

The corners of his eyes crinkled, but his smile was bittersweet. "My mom would've liked you. She never wanted us to miss a chance to be kids."

It was clear the grief from losing his parents was still potent. Somehow, she'd stepped closer to him, reached for his hand. He clasped her hand easily, naturally. As if they'd held hands for years. His fingers threaded through hers, and a zing of emotion triggered inside her gut.

"I would've liked the chance to meet her," she said softly.

His smile was tight, and she didn't miss emotion in his eyes.

He cleared his throat. "If you're only giving Evan half an hour, he might need help to get his fort done."

Her brows went up. "You really want to build a snow fort?"

"Sure. I'm rusty but I think I can handle it."

She examined his face for any sign of impure motives. "Why?"

He tugged her slightly closer, let his opposite hand come up so that his fingertips touched her waist. "Because I want to know you. And he's a part of you."

Breath caught in her throat. The way he was looking at her...

She was helpless against the emotion rising inside her. He dipped his head forward, and she rose up on tiptoe to meet his kiss.

His lips brushed hers. Once. Again. She felt the brush of his scruff where he hadn't shaved this morning, the tip of his nose against her cheek.

He settled into the kiss, as if he had all the time in the world, as if there wasn't a little boy in the other room, ready to burst in on them.

She was the one who felt as if she were coming out of her own skin and helpless to stop.

He moved back slightly, only a breath between them. At her waist, his fingertips brushed gently.

What am I doing?

"You're a million miles away," he whispered, his breath fanning her lips.

She wasn't. She was glued to the floor, her heart beating a panicky rhythm.

He must've caught Evan's pounding footsteps a fraction of a second before she did, because he steadied her even as he stepped back.

The concern on his expression only made the knot in her stomach worse.

She turned her face away, turned to Evan on the pretense of making sure he was bundled enough. "Hat?"

"Mo-om," her son complained.

His beanie was already on.

"You mind if I take a shot at building that fort with you?" Cash asked.

"Really? Sure!"

She tugged on her son's zipper, stalling for time before she had to look back at the man.

When she did, Cash only winked at her and made for his coveralls and boots.

"So how do you want to do this?" Cash asked.

He stood just steps from the stoop of Delaney's house, Evan beside him, both of them squinting in the sun's glare off the pristine blanket of snow.

"Find a good snowbank and dig in," Cash asked, "or go with snow bricks and build from the ground up?"

The boy's head tilted to the side as he gave

serious consideration to the yard. "Snow bricks," he decided.

Cash nodded. "My sister and I did a big one, once. I was about... your age." He knelt in the snow and started scooping handfuls to himself. "Why don't you pace off an outline of where you want each wall to be. I'll start making bricks."

He caught Delaney's shadow in the big picture window. She was sipping a mug of coffee. And probably watching every move he made with her kid.

He'd freaked her out with his kiss. He'd been sure she'd wanted it. It'd been there in her eyes, in the way her body had swayed toward him... but then when he'd delivered, he'd felt tension overtake her. Like her mind had been elsewhere.

Not his best performance if he couldn't keep her attention with his kiss.

Maybe it was because Evan was in the house. It wasn't an ideal place for a first kiss, not super romantic, but he was working with what he had.

Maybe he just needed to be a little more patient. Like when breaking a skittish horse. Move too fast, and you were bucked off, rear end sore from hitting the ground.

Evan stomped a decent-sized circle in the ground, laughing when snow when flying.

Cash finished pounding a third brick into shape as the boy trekked through the shin-high snow to him. "Igloo shape, nice."

"The roof will probably be the hardest part," Evan said. "I watched some YouTube videos, and I think I can do it."

Good for you, kid.

Evan knelt in the snow next to Cash and watched as he formed a six inch square brick. The snow was perfect for building, just moist enough to stick together. Cash started on his own brick.

"Were you kissing my mom?" Evan asked, his head down.

Shoot. Cash had hoped he'd reacted quickly enough to keep the boy from seeing the embrace. He wasn't ashamed of it, not at all, but what should he say to Evan?

He went with the truth. "Yeah."

"Oh." Evan squinted up at him. His hat had slid over one eyebrow, which made Cash want to smile, but the boy was so serious. "Do you like her? You know, *like* like her?"

Cash let his gloved hand rest on top of the

brick he'd been working on and gave the boy his full attention. "I haven't known your mom very long, but I think she's pretty awesome."

Evan nodded. "She is."

Cash had to smile at the boy's quick agreement.

Evan pounded another brick into shape. "She doesn't date."

Cash lifted a brick in each hand and moved to the outline Evan had created. "Because of your dad?"

Evan followed, carting a big brick. He placed it next to the two Cash had laid. "Because she works *all* the time. And when she's not working, she takes care of me. Takes me to doctors appointments and stuff. Sometimes I get sick and throw up."

The boy looked down. "I wish she didn't have to."

He put a hand on Evan's shoulder, conscious of how bony it was. "Your treatments won't last forever, will they?"

Evan shook his head, still looking down.

Cash considered for a moment. "Maybe if you guys had someone else who could help, your mom wouldn't be so stressed out." And Evan wouldn't have to feel guilty.

Evan squinted up at him again. "You must really like my mom if you want to clean up vomit for her."

Cash couldn't help a chuckle. Was he that crazy for Delaney? Yeah. He really was. "My dad once told me that when I met the right woman for me, I'd know it. And your mom knocked me on my rear last night. I think she's the one."

Evan looked up at him, expression serious. "She might try to talk you out of liking her."

Perceptive kid.

Cash grinned at him. "You want to know what training a horse is like?"

DELANEY RUSHED through the quickest shower in mankind, followed by a high-powered blow-dry before she threw on a pair of jeans and a cashmere sweater she'd found at Goodwill, which was a little more flattering than her PJs.

She brushed on a smear of lip gloss and quickly applied eye makeup.

She'd watched the two males for a few minutes before ducking into the bathroom and spent at least twenty minutes on her abbreviated beauty routine, so she rushed back to the living room in bare feet.

The boys were still outside.

She stood at the window again, watching as Cash placed the last brick carefully on the roof of the igloo-slash-snow fort. Evan was sitting inside, and she could hear his chatter through the windowpane, though she couldn't make out his words.

Cash answered, his voice deeper but his words no clearer.

She lifted her hand to knock on the glass and call them inside—she couldn't risk Evan's health—but suddenly a snowball flew out of the igloo and hit Cash's pant leg.

She saw the man pause, glance at her briefly. As far as she could tell, the attack from Evan had been unprovoked.

Cash held up two fingers, mouthed *two minutes*. And then knelt and scooped a handful of snow, quickly packing it into a ball.

She watched the fight unfold, Evan tossing ball after ball that he must've squirreled away in the fort. Most of Cash's shots hit the igloo. Was he purposely missing her son?

Finally, Evan launched a last barrage and then fell out of the igloo, laughing so hard he was holding his sides.

Cash was laughing, too, carefree and full, the sound audible through the glass. Hearing it made her stomach swoop.

Cash was too perfect. He liked her son. Owned a huge ranch and didn't have to worry about money. Was as handsome as a movie star.

How could she even think she'd hold his interest for more than a minute?

Cash ruffled the top of Evan's head and pointed toward the house. They both stomped snow off their feet on the stoop. She held the door open and shivered when a rush of cold air hit the still-damp nape of her neck.

"Freeze," she told Evan. She pointed to the huge beach towel she'd pulled out of the closet. "Shoes. Coat."

She helped him pull off the snow-encrusted coat, getting a shower of snow for her trouble. His hair was mussed from the beanie. She felt his forehead where it'd been beneath the hat. Cool but not too bad.

"Mom," he protested, shifting away with a glance at Cash.

"You can give me a check," the rancher said with a slow grin as he slid the coveralls down his arms and waist.

Evan barked a laugh as she felt heat spreading across her chest. The hunter-green sweater she'd chosen had a V-neck, and she knew pink must be showing there when Cash gave an obvious glance and then smirked.

She slapped his bicep. Playfully.

She pointed at Evan. "Go change your clothes and then come back to the kitchen for some hot chocolate."

"Aw, Mom. I'm not a baby."

"No, but I bet your socks and pants are wet."

Evan trudged across the room. "You didn't start putting together my track, did you?"

"I just opened the box," she said.

"Mom has to have supervision for anything that requires assembly," Evan threw over his shoulder.

"Hey!" she cried.

Too late. Cash's eyes were laughing as he stripped the coverall pants down his legs and off.

"I'm pretty handy," he offered as he straightened. "You can supervise me all you want."

The innuendo in his words made the heat

across her chest flare hotter. She crossed her arms in mock indignation.

"Don't you have to go home?" she asked tartly.

The laughter in his eyes died away. "You ready for me to go?"

She shrugged. "I'm sure you and your sister have plans for the holiday, don't you?"

He smirked again, but this time not at her expense. "My sister got the Christmas gift she really wanted. Maverick, my best friend," he explained. "He's in the marines, and his leave is up tomorrow. I'm pretty sure Mallory hasn't given me a thought all day."

"Ah." Lucky girl.

"So can I stay? If I promise to keep my lips to myself and not to freak you out again?"

She was burning up. Needed to trade her sweater for a T-shirt. "You noticed?"

He winced slightly. "Hard not to. It's been a while since I kissed anyone. I'm probably as rusty at that as I am at building a snow fort."

"I haven't kissed anyone since Jonah," she admitted softly. "And... what are we doing here?" she dared speak the words out loud. "What is it you're hoping happens after today? I'm not exactly dating material."

He nodded, totally unsurprised. "Evan told me."

She was taken aback.

He advanced on her, didn't stop until he was leaning over her, supporting himself with one arm braced on the wall above her head. "He said you work yourself to exhaustion, and when you're not working, you're all about keeping him healthy."

"He did not," she breathed. It was hard to catch her breath with him so close.

He ignored her. "He also said you'd try to talk me out of pursuing you."

She considered taking back the presents from beneath the tree.

"Don't you think we're too different to make a relationship work?" she asked.

"Because you're a city girl and I'm a country boy?" he asked.

"No. You know why."

"Because you're a busy single mom and I'm in between jobs right now?"

Hot anger surged. "No," she said sharply. "Because I clean your house—mansion. And others' houses. Because people like you treat people like me like... like that guy last night.

Because I'm not the same as you."

He leaned back, put distance between them. "I would never have treated you or anyone like that."

She folded her arms over her middle. "No. To behave like that, you'd have to notice me. And most people in your social circles only notice me when the cleaning isn't done right."

"Yesterday, my behavior had nothing to do with you. It's hard to take over your father's business. My dad... he was so good at running the ranch, and I always feel one step behind. Like I'll never measure up. The way I treated you was unthinkable, and I'm sorry. But it had nothing to do with you."

She shook her head, feeling guilty for bringing it up again. He'd already apologized and she'd forgiven him.

...But couldn't he see how unequal they were? He'd never understand...

When he spoke again, his voice was quiet and serious. "As far as I'm concerned, I'm a man and you're a woman. Who cares what our annual salaries are?"

"I do!" she blurted. Couldn't he see how unequal they were? He'd never understand why she had to work so much, not when money came so easily to him. Or what about...? "When your birthday comes, what happens when I can't afford a gift for you?" Those things seemed small, but they added up.

She knew. She'd grown up with a maid for a mom. How many times had she worn clothes from Goodwill when her friends at school had brand new things?

He had a little crease between his eyebrows. "I guess I wouldn't care."

"Yes, you would," she snapped. Why couldn't he see what she did?

"Then I guess I'd like it if you made me a special dinner," he said with an easy shrug.

She growled.

It didn't faze him. "When we're married, our incomes will be combined," he said easily.

"What?" she yelped.

And of course, Evan chose that moment to burst back into the room, sliding on the old wood floors in his sock feet. "Is the hot chocolate ready?"

CHAPTER 7

IT WAS EIGHT O'CLOCK WHEN THEIR CHRISTMAS movie marathon ended and Evan asked if he could read in his room.

She gave him a kiss and let him go, knowing he'd be sound asleep on the bed when she went to tuck him in later.

She was thankful for the chemo, thankful the cancer was disappearing—if slowly—from his body. But his energy wasn't what it used to be. Would he ever be back to normal?

Cash sat on the opposite end of the sofa, long legs stretched out in front of him, one arm stretched across the back of the sofa. He'd been playing with her hair while the movie rolled. He looked relaxed, but she knew the power he'd leashed. He reminded her of a lion at rest.

She remembered thinking last night that his smile was the smile of a man used to getting what he wanted.

And she still hadn't been able to reconcile how a relationship between them would work.

"Do you want some more coffee?" she asked. Sudden nerves sent her up off the sofa.

Cash sat forward, placing his palms on his knees. "You got any tea?"

"Iced tea?"

"Hot." A smile spread across his mouth. "You don't think a rancher should drink hot tea? You're painting me with an awful masculine brush."

"I'm just surprised," she said.

He'd been surprising her all day, from the moment she'd opened the door to him.

She hurried into the kitchen and rummaged under the cabinets until she came up with the teakettle she'd used maybe once in her married life. She filled it and put it on the stove.

She sensed Cash follow her into the kitchen. He stood in the same spot he had earlier, one shoulder propped against the archway. This time he faced into the kitchen, watching her again.

Those butterflies he'd inspired came to life in

her belly again. She turned to the upper cabinet to look for the tea bags—hopefully they were still good. She'd bought them once after Sierra had told her the tea would help her sleep. It hadn't.

And then because he was still watching her, still not saying anything, she ran some hot water for the dishes still on the counter from their meal earlier.

Plunging her hands into the soapy water, she could let herself focus on the task. Not the man. She'd give herself five minutes to try and regain equilibrium.

It wouldn't work, but she'd try.

It had been an incredible day. After the snow fort, she'd lugged out the small toolkit she kept beneath the kitchen sink and read the directions as the two males had assembled Evan's racetrack. They'd run races for nearly an hour, had only quit when she'd served lunch.

She and Evan had introduced Cash to their family tradition of having hamburgers for their special meal. Cash had manned the grill, skipping the coveralls to hurry out and back inside in his coat and boots. It had been bittersweet for her, remembering Jonah doing the same thing on another frigid Christmas. Evan hadn't remembered when she'd mentioned it. Maybe he'd been too young.

During the meal, Cash had regaled them with stories of his childhood Christmases spent with parents and grandparents at the Double Cross. His grandparents had died when he was a teen, and now his parents were gone too. He hadn't hidden the huskiness in his voice. Once, he'd wiped a tear from beneath his eyes. She didn't know what to do with the honest vulnerability he kept showing her.

It had been different with Jonah. They'd dated for months before they'd really opened up with each other and shared heartbreaks. Even after they'd been married, when things were difficult at work or some stressor was getting to him, Jonah would mostly keep that to himself.

Not Cash.

He wasn't afraid to let her know how he felt. And apparently, he felt a lot after only a day of being acquainted with her.

When we get married.

His teasing words from earlier had resurfaced in her brain during the most unexpected times throughout the day, ping-ponging through her thoughts and scattering them.

He *had been* teasing when he'd said it. She was sure of it.

Mostly.

He had sounded awfully sure of himself for someone who'd just met her yesterday.

And this line of thinking wasn't helping calm her butterflies whatsoever.

"Are you really going to ride that souped-up golf cart home?" she asked. The window over the sink showed a reflection of the kitchen, since it was dark outside, but in true Texas fashion, the temps outside had been rising all day, and the snow had melted into mush. So far, Evan's igloo was still intact, but it wouldn't last long.

"It's a utility vehicle," he said. "And yeah. With the sun down, the roads'll be slick in some places. I'll be all right."

She placed the last spoon in the drying rack and reached for the dish towel to dry her hands. Just in time, because the teakettle whistled.

She opened the drawer where she kept the dish towels and pot holders, and a loose piece of paper crinkled.

She ignored, whipping out a potholder to take the teakettle off the burner. She poured the steaming water into Cash's mug over the teabag.

And then went back to the drawer. She'd shoved the stack of bills that usually graced the kitchen counter into the drawer two days ago, not wanting to see them on Christmas Day. She'd wanted one day of peace. Had the day's cooking and dishwashing displaced something? She couldn't afford to lose even one bill.

But when her glance fell to the drawer, the paper she saw there wasn't an eight-by-eleven sheet, wasn't a printed bill. It was a check. Loose in the drawer.

"What is this?" She glanced at Cash and then reached for it.

He came off the wall, stepped toward her. "I kinda hoped you wouldn't find that until tomorrow."

Find *what*?

She picked it up, turned it over. Gasped. "You wrote me a check for twenty-five grand?"

She dropped it on the island counter as if it'd burned her fingertips. Her hands were shaking. "I don't get it."

He came around the island, hands outstretched as he reached for her. She backed away.

He stopped, shoved his hands into his jeans'

pockets. "I accidentally saw your stack of bills when I was doing the dishes this morning. I wasn't snooping. Much."

She pressed her shaking fingers to her eyes. "So... what? You decided to pop off a check for *twenty-five k?*"

Who had that kind of money in their checking account?

Not her.

She'd been pretending all day. Allowing herself to suspend disbelief—like when she watched a TV show or movie that was a little too far-fetched.

But the check lying out on the empty counter was too much.

It'd broken the tiny shield she'd been using to allow herself to pretend that this thing with Cash could work out.

DELANEY WAS FREAKING OUT AGAIN. This time it was for sure Cash's fault.

He'd left the check with pure intentions. He didn't want her stressed out about money, not when Evan needed her.

But her tossing the check as if it were a tarantula hadn't been how he'd envisioned her finding out.

His hands itched to reach for her where she stood in the corner where the two walls of cabinets met. She was trembling, pressing her fingertips into her eyes.

But he kept his hands in his pockets. His skittish filly had backed away.

And he didn't want her to send him home, not yet. Not when she was worked up like this.

"It's just money," he said. "I want to help—"

She laughed, an edge of hysteria to it. When she brought her hands away from her face, her eyes were red-rimmed. "*It's just money*. Spoken like someone who has never had to worry where their next meal will come from. Or wonder if the electric company will cancel your service *today* or *tomorrow*."

The little hairs on the back of his nape stood to attention. He had never been in either of those situations. He wouldn't apologize for his life. It was just how things were. And if what she described was her reality, she *should* take the money.

"It's not a big deal," he said.

She laughed that not-laugh again. "To you!"

She crossed her arms over her middle, which made him want to pull her close even more. "I don't want you to fix this!"

"Like you didn't want me to fix things last night when that jerk assaulted you?" He'd meant to say the words calmly, but thinking about what had almost happened last night had him seeing red all over again.

She went still. "That's not—" She shook her head, almost seeming to clutch herself with her arms.

He hadn't meant to upset her.

She breathed in deeply. "That's not the same."

"What was it, then?" he asked, because he hadn't understood last night, and he still didn't.

She looked at him silently.

"Was it because of Evan? Are you somehow trying to protect him? Because I'm sure he'd want to see that guy pay for what he did."

Fire sparked in her eyes. "If I make trouble, I'll lose clients I can't afford to lose."

Make trouble. As if she were the one who'd invited it. "That won't happen," he said.

She looked at him so incredulously that it hurt. "I know these things," she said softly. "My mama cleaned houses. She taught me everything she knew. Be discreet. Be invisible, if you can. Apologize. Clients don't want a housekeeper who makes trouble."

That hurt, deep inside. Knowing she believed she had to take whatever was dished out by the people who paid her.

And he'd perpetuated it with his own behavior yesterday. He'd been unthinking and ignorant.

"I'm sorry," he said, because he really was. He hated it for her. "Isn't that a reason to take the money?"

She reached over to the counter and picked up the check, crumbling it in her fist. Then she fired it at him. It hit his chest and fell to the floor.

"You don't get it at all," she said. She sounded so desolate.

And he was afraid that if he said the wrong thing now, he was going to lose her forever. "Help me understand."

"If I'm the kind of person you have to *fix*..." She breathed in deep through her nose. "Do you really think you want to be with someone needy like me? In the long run?"

That was what she thought?

"Honey..." He really needed to touch her. She

was still so wound up, her shoulders hunched, her stance tense.

He took his hands out of his pockets and held them out, palms upraised.

She hesitated. He waited.

And then she unwound her arms from around her middle and tentatively placed her palms in his.

"I'm not some perfect person," he started. "Sometimes I need help, too. We all do. After my parents died, I fell into a black hole. I couldn't eat. Couldn't sleep. It took Mallory and a therapist to pull me out of that gully of grief. I still get stuck in the mud of it sometimes. Like yesterday."

He squeezed her hands gently. "If I've got money in the bank, and I can help you, then I want to. That's what—" He re-adjusted mid-sentence. "That's what friends do." He'd almost said, *that's what people who love each other do.*

She frowned down at their linked hands. "So you give me money and I give you emotional support," she asked skeptically.

He shook her hands. "I would have given up anything—any amount of cash, my own life—to have my parents back. They were amazing—the love they shared was so strong... That's what I think you and I can have."

After too many seconds, she looked up at him with uncertainty, hope. And then she closed her eyes. She pulled her hands away and retreated. All the way into the living room, leaving him standing alone in the kitchen.

DELANEY STOOD in front of the Christmas tree, arms again around her middle, hands clasping her elbows.

She felt as if she would fly apart at any moment.

What Cash was offering... She wanted it. So badly.

To lean on him. Let him bear some of her burdens. Not even the money, though that was nice. The man, standing beside her. Holding her hand when she had a tough meeting with one of Evan's doctors.

She'd been alone since Jonah's death. Even before that, she hadn't felt she could trust him with her most tender feelings, her fears.

What Cash was asking her to share was maybe the scariest thing she'd ever done.

She didn't know if she could.

She didn't have to turn around to know the moment he walked into the room behind her. Would she always carry this awareness of him?

He came closer, stood behind her. Not touching.

He cleared his throat. "Do you want me to leave?"

She squeezed her eyes closed against the colorful glow of the tree lights.

"Do you remember when you were a kid?" she whispered in answer. "It was so easy to believe that Christmas could bring miracles. Real ones."

He was so close she could feel the warmth from his big body. Still, he didn't touch her.

She opened her eyes, and the colorful lights blurred through the tears that gathered in her eyes. "Last year, Evan had just been diagnosed. All I wanted for Christmas was for my boy to *live*."

Cash was quiet. Listening.

"I don't know if I can believe in Christmas miracles anymore," she admitted in a whisper.

"Do you want to?"

She turned and found him there. It was easy to burrow into his arms, easier than she'd thought it would be. She pressed her face into his shoulder. Nodded.

She wanted to believe. "I'm scared," she whispered into his shirt.

He held her tightly, one big hand cupping the back of her head. "Then I'll believe enough for the both of us. For now."

He held her until her quaking stopped. Until her breathing evened out and the tears that had threatened passed.

He kissed her temple. "We had a good day, didn't we?" His words were murmured into her hair.

"Yes, but—"

He waited for her to finish.

"But Christmas is an anomaly," she said. "Tomorrow, I'll go back to work. Things will go back to normal."

And she was afraid he wouldn't like her normal.

"We'll make it work," he said. "I'm not going back to Austin for a job. Not yet." He kissed her ear this time. "I can cart Evan to some of his appointments. Pick him up from school. Make dinner. Keep hounding you to let me pay some of his medical bills."

She squeezed her eyes closed against another onset of tears.

"Why?" she choked out.

"Because you're it for me."

He gently nudged her chin up with one hand. She opened her eyes, and a tear fell, dripping down her cheek. He caught it with his thumb.

"You don't even know me," she whispered.

"I know enough. My dad believed in love at first sight, because he'd experienced it. Now I have, too."

Love.

He'd said the word. The one that seemed impossible. It wasn't possible, was it?

His hand slid to cup her jaw. "Is there any chance Evan is going to wake up and interrupt us again?"

His intent was clear. He was going to kiss her. She wanted him to.

"There's always a chance." It was the reality of life with a child.

One corner of his lip quirked. "I'll risk it."

This time when his lips brushed hers, all thought fled. Everything except the heat of his mouth, the taste of him, the feel of his hand at her waist.

She didn't want to be anywhere else.

She was going to take the risk, too.

When he'd made her appropriately breathless, he moved back to brush a kiss on her cheek. "I'm falling in love with you," he whispered.

Her soul took flight, and powerful emotion spiraled through her. So sweet that she had to close her eyes against it.

He kissed her jaw. "I'll keep saying it until you believe, too."

"Okay," she agreed in a whisper.

And it was enough, because he kissed her again.

❄

FIND out what happens with Cash and Delaney on Christmas Eve one year later… get the bonus story Christmas Ever After.

ALSO BY LACY WILLIAMS

SNOWBOUND IN SAWYER CREEK SERIES (CONTEMPORARY ROMANCE)

Soldier Under the Mistletoe

The Nanny's Christmas Wish

The Rancher's Unexpected Gift

WILD WYOMING HEART SERIES (HISTORICAL ROMANCE)

Marrying Miss Marshal

Counterfeit Cowboy

Cowboy Pride

Courted by a Cowboy

TRIPLE H BRIDES SERIES (CONTEMPORARY ROMANCE)

Kissing Kelsey

Courting Carrie

Stealing Sarah

Keeping Kayla

Melting Megan

COWBOY FAIRYTALES SERIES (CONTEMPORARY ROMANCE)

Once Upon a Cowboy

Cowboy Charming

The Toad Prince

The Beastly Princess

The Lost Princess

HEART OF OKLAHOMA SERIES (CONTEMPORARY ROMANCE)

Kissed by a Cowboy

Love Letters from Cowboy

Mistletoe Cowboy

Cowgirl for Keeps

Jingle Bell Cowgirl

Heart of a Cowgirl

3 Days with a Cowboy

Prodigal Cowgirl

WYOMING LEGACY SERIES (HISTORICAL ROMANCE)

The Homesteader's Sweetheart

Roping the Wrangler

Return of the Cowboy Doctor

The Wrangler's Inconvenient Wife

A Cowboy for Christmas

Her Convenient Cowboy

Her Cowboy Deputy

NOT IN A SERIES

How to Lose a Guy in 10 Dates

Santa Next Door

The Butterfly Bride

Secondhand Cowboy

Wagon Train Sweetheart (historical romance)

88155211R00074

Made in the USA
Columbia, SC
01 February 2018